SUN & MOON

Fairy Tales From Korea

ADAPTED BY KATHLEEN SEROS

ILLUSTRATED BY
NORMAN SIBLEY & ROBERT KRAUSE

HOLLYM

contents

First published in 1982
Twelfth printing, 1996
by Hollym International Corp.
18 Donald Place, Elizabeth, New Jersey 07208 U.S.A.
Phone: (908) 353-1655   Fax: (908) 353-0255

Published simultaneously in Korea
by Hollym Corporation; Publishers
14-5 Kwanchol-dong, Chongno-gu, Seoul 110-111, Korea
Phone: (02) 735-7554   Fax: (02) 730-5149

ISBN: 0-930878-25-6

Library of Congress Catalog Card Number: 82-82510

Printed in Korea

For Carrie and Kate

sun
and
moon

Once upon a time, a widow woman lived in the mountains with her son and daughter. Each day, the woman went to the village to work in a nobleman's house in order to feed her children.

One night, as she was returning home, a tiger jumped out onto the path and said, "Old woman, what are you carrying on your head?"

"A basket of buckwheat puddings for dinner," she replied.

"If you don't give me one, I'll eat you up," the tiger growled. So she gave him a pudding and went on her way.

But the tiger was greedy. He ran ahead and jumped out from behind a hill and stopped the woman again. "Old woman, give me a pudding or I'll eat you up," he roared. And so she did and went on her way.

But the tiger was not content and he stopped her again and again in the same way until he had eaten all of her puddings. With the empty basket on her head, she went on her way.

The tiger ran ahead and once more jumped out onto the path and demanded a pudding. "You greedy old tiger," she cried. "You've eaten all my puddings! What can I do?"

"Give me your arms or I'll eat you all up," he replied. And so she gave the tiger her arms and went on her way.

But the tiger stopped her again and said, "I'm still hungry, old woman. Give me your legs or I'll eat you all up." She gave him her legs and, rolling over and over, she went on her way.

But the evil tiger ran after her once more and gobbled up the rest of her in a single gulp!

Back home, the children waited for their mother to come home. When it got dark, they went inside and locked the door, for they remembered her warnings to be careful of the tigers who lived in the mountains. They were very hungry but there was no food, so they lay down on the floor and waited for their mother to bring supper.

Meanwhile, the tiger had dressed himself in the poor woman's clothes and, thinking what a tasty dessert the children would make, went to their house.

He stood on his hind legs and knocked on the door. "Open the door, my dears, Mother is home," he said. "I've brought you some buckwheat puddings."

"Mother, your voice sounds so strange. Is it really you?" the children asked.

"Of course, children. I've spent the day chasing sparrows away from the barley drying on the mats, so my voice is rather hoarse," the tiger replied.

But the children were not convinced so they said, "Mother, please put your arm through the hole in the door and let us

11

see it." When the tiger put one of his paws through the hole, the children felt it and asked, "Mother, why is your arm so very rough?"

"I had to do the laundry today and I starched the clothes with rice paste. That must have made my arm so rough," explained the tiger.

But the children still were not convinced so they peeked out through the hole in the door and saw the big tiger standing there. Needless to say, they were very frightened but they were also very clever. They quickly ran outside through the back door, climbed the big tree near the water well and quietly hid in the branches.

Again, the tiger asked the children to open the door but, of course, there was no answer. Finally, he became so angry that he forced open the door and rushed into the house.

When he realized that he had been tricked, he burst into a furious rage and roared terrible roars. He searched everywhere for the children all through the night but he could not find them.

The next morning, the weary tiger sat down by the well to rest. As it became light, he saw the reflections of the boy and girl in the water of the well. Thinking that they were hiding inside, he said, "Oh, my poor children. You've fallen into the well. I must rescue you."

The children were watching from high up in the tree and could not stop themselves from laughing at the stupid tiger. Hearing their laughter, the tiger looked up and discovered their hiding place.

"Oh, my poor children. You're stuck up in the tree. How can I rescue you?" he said.

"Get some sesame oil and smear it on the tree trunk. That will make it easy for you to climb up," they replied.

The tiger ran and got a jug of sesame oil and rubbed it all over the tree trunk but, of course, the oil made it very slippery. Although he tried again and again, he could not climb up.

Then the tiger walked a short distance away from the tree. He ran toward the tree as fast as he could and took a giant leap. But he could not quite reach the first branch and although he clawed at it frantically, he finally fell to the ground in a heap.

Rubbing his bruises, the tiger slowly got up and said, "You certainly are clever children. However did you get to the top of this tree?"

But this time the children were not so clever and answered, "If you get an axe, you can use it to cut notches in the trunk to use as steps." The tiger did just that and began climbing up the tree.

As the tiger climbed closer and closer, the terrified children realized they could never escape and called out, "Heavenly King, now we will surely die! If we are worthy, please save us."

At once, the Heavenly Iron Chain descended from the sky. The children quickly climbed onto the chain and it gently pulled them up through the clouds to the Heavenly Kingdom.

The frustrated tiger then prayed, "Heavenly King, please send the Heavenly Iron Chain for me, too." But the Heavenly King sent the Rotten Straw Rope down to the tiger instead. The tiger grabbed onto the rope anyway and it slowly pulled him up toward the Heavenly Kingdom. But, when it was half way up, the rope broke and the tiger crashed to earth and splattered into a million pieces.

It was beautiful in the Heavenly Kingdom and the boy and girl lived happily there. One day, the Heavenly King came to them and said, "Children, you have had time for a good rest but no one may remain idle here in the Heavenly Kingdom. It is time for you each to perform a special task."

The Heavenly King decided to make the little boy the moon to shine at night and the little girl the sun to light the world by day.

It is told that when she became the sun, the people on earth often looked at her in the sky. But she was a modest girl so she shone more and more brightly until it was impossible to look at her directly. And that is why the sun is so bright.

the woodcutter and the heavenly maiden

There once was a handsome young woodcutter who lived with his mother in the forest. He was so poor that he could not take a bride but he never complained about his misfortune.

One day, as he was working in the mountains, a terrified young deer came running up to him. "Please help me!" the creature begged. "Hide me or else I'll soon be killed."

The gentle woodcutter quickly hid the deer beneath a pile of fallen leaves. At once, a hunter with a bow and arrow ran up to him. "I've been chasing a deer. Have you seen it?" asked the hunter.

"Oh, yes," replied the woodcutter, "it ran past here and down into that valley." The hunter rushed off in pursuit.

The grateful deer came out from under the leaves and told the woodcutter that she was a servant of the God of the Mountain. "You have saved my life," she said. "To repay your kindness, I will tell you something that will bring you great happiness."

"Climb up Diamond Mountain tomorrow afternoon," she continued, "and go to the lake between the peaks at the foot of the rainbow. Hide yourself in the bushes and, at two o'clock, eight Heavenly Maidens will come to bathe in the lake. While they are bathing, you must hide the silken garments belonging to one of them. Without them, she will not be able to return to Heaven."

"When the others leave, go and welcome her and she will return home with you. She will become your wife and bear your children and you will live happily ever after. But you must not return her silken clothes until you have had four children." And with those words, the deer vanished.

Early the next morning, the woodcutter climbed the great mountain. It was the most beautiful in the land with crystal clear lakes and waterfalls, dense pine forests and deep valleys covered with mist. Here, the great mountain peaks touched the blue sky and the singing of birds could be heard everywhere.

When he reached the highest lake, the woodcutter hid behind a tree. Precisely at two o'clock, eight Heavenly Maidens came floating down to earth on the rainbow. They chatted merrily as they hung their clothes on the branches of pine trees and jumped into the lake to bathe.

The man was spellbound by their heavenly beauty but finally remembered the deer's instructions. He quickly took one of the silken garments and, carefully folding it, put it in his pocket and hid himself again.

When the maidens finished bathing and began to get dressed, they were most upset to discover that the clothes of the youngest maiden were missing. They searched high and

low but could not find them. At sunset, they had to return home before the Heavenly Gates were closed. Waving good-bye, they floated back up into the sky on the rainbow, leaving the youngest behind.

She lay crying on the ground as the woodcutter approached. Although frightened of the man, she was struck at once by his handsomeness. He apologized sincerely for the trouble he had caused her and was so kind and gentle that she agreed to go home with him and become his wife.

They were married and lived very happily. The woodcutter worked hard in the forest all day and his wife tended the house and was a good mother to their three children.

One day, she asked, "My dear husband, it's been so very long since I've seen my silken clothes. Won't you please show them to me?"

The man loved his wife with all his heart and felt sorry that he had kept the clothes hidden from her. Disregarding the deer's advice, he brought them to her. She put the garments on and at once felt an uncontrollable longing to return to Heaven. Having regained her magical powers, she slowly floated up to Heaven with the children in her arms as her husband watched helplessly.

The woodcutter was overcome by grief and spent each day in the forest gazing at the sky and longing for his family. One day, the deer which he had saved many years before appeared and he told his sad tale to her.

"You didn't follow my instructions," she said, "but you saved my life and I will help you. Go again to the lake on Diamond Mountain. Ever since you took the Heavenly Maiden's clothes, they do not go there to bathe. Instead, each day they send down a golden bucket from Heaven and draw water from the lake. When the bucket appears, climb inside and you will be pulled up to Heaven."

The woodcutter did exactly what the deer had told him and was carried up to Heaven in the golden bucket. The Heavenly King gave permission for him to stay and the family was overjoyed to be reunited. Heaven was beautiful beyond belief. They had the most exquisite clothes to wear and the most delicious food to eat and they lived very happily.

One day, the woodcutter thought of his old mother living alone back on earth and told his wife that he wanted to go to visit her. She did not want him to go because he was still a mortal being but he finally convinced her to let him go.

"I will summon a dragon-horse for you and it will take you back to earth in the twinkling of an eye," she said. "But, dear husband, you must take care not to touch the ground for, if you do, you will never be able to return to Heaven." The woodcutter promised to be careful as he mounted the dragon-horse, and then they flew to earth in an instant.

The mother was very happy to see her son again and they had a wonderful visit. As he was preparing to leave, she said, "Dear son, before you go, please have a bowl of your favorite pumpkin porridge."

He could not refuse her kind offer and he took the bowl of piping hot porridge. But the bowl was too hot for him to hold and he accidentally dropped it on the back of the dragon-horse. The frightened animal reared up on his hind legs in pain, throwing the man to the ground, and flew off to Heaven.

Now the woodcutter could never go back to Heaven. He stood outside every day and looked up at the sky, calling to his wife and children. After many years, he was transformed into a rooster and it is said that is why to this very day roosters crow with their necks stretched toward Heaven.

It is also said that the Heavenly Maidens now bathe in the Milky Way and their splashing is what makes the rainbows on earth.

the nine-headed giant

In ancient times, there was a giant with nine heads who lived far off in the mountains. Every so often, he would go to the closest village and snatch away one of the villagers. All the people were terrified but there was nothing that they could do.

One day, the giant came and carried away a beautiful young woman and her maid-servant. When her husband heard the terrible news, he immediately set off to the mountains to rescue them.

Deep in the woods, the man met an old woman who lived in a small, thatched cottage. "Do you know where the nine-headed giant lives?" he asked.

"Yes," she replied, "but he is very, very strong. If you are going to fight him you must first eat this magic ginseng root."

After he ate the root, the woman said, "Now go and lift that big stone over there." The man tried, but he could hardly move it. She gave him another ginseng root to eat and he found that he could lift the stone up to his knees. The old woman gave him a third root and he was able to lift the huge stone over his head without difficulty.

"I think you are strong enough to kill him now," she said. Then she gave him a sword and told him, "Go over the next hill and look for a great, flat stone. Lift up the stone and you will see the entrance to a cave. Inside, there is a path which will take you to the home of the giant."

The man went over the hill and found the stone. He moved it aside and entered the cave. The path led him down and down into the underworld. Finally, he came upon a huge, tiled house surrounded by a stone wall with nine gates. He crept through a gate into the courtyard and quickly climbed up into a willow tree beside a well.

In a short while, a woman came to draw water from the well and the man could see that she was his own wife's maid-servant. When she had filled the jar with water, he dropped some leaves into the water. She scooped out the leaves and filled the jar again. He dropped more leaves into the jar.

"It seems quite breezy today," she grumbled. Again she re-filled the jar and the man again dropped some leaves into the water. At last, she looked up into the tree and saw him. "Master!" she cried, "come quickly and I will take you to your wife."

The maid-servant led him to a secret room inside the house and summoned her mistress who was filled with joy by the sight of her husband.

She began to tell him all about the dreadful giant. "His habits are quite peculiar," she explained. "He goes away for three months and ten days. After he returns, he sleeps for three months and ten days. He'll be back in three months time. In the meantime, you must grow even stronger or you'll never be able to defeat him."

She led her husband to a hidden cave. Inside, there was a spring with magical water as clear as crystal. "This water will help strengthen you," she told him. "You must drink it every day until the giant returns."

After a week, she brought a huge sword to him. "This is the giant's sword," she said. "Can you use it?" He tried but it was too heavy. But after a few more weeks, he was strong enough to use the sword with ease.

In one month, he was strong enough to wear the giant's huge shoes and could even jump high in the air as he wore them.

After two months, he could swing the giant's great spiked war club around and around in circles in the air.

When three months had passed, he was so strong that he was able to wear the giant's tremendous helmet and armor and carry two swords as well.

One day, the air was filled with a deafening sound—it was the giant's thunderous footsteps. The noise got louder and louder and, with an ear-splitting stamp, the horrible giant appeared at the gate. He marched into the courtyard and roared, "I smell a man!"

The young woman replied, "Oh no, master. There are no men here. You must be very tired after your long journey. Come—I have prepared special food and wine for you."

The giant went inside and ate all the food which she brought to him. And he drank nine big barrels of wine—one with each mouth! Afterward, he lay down and fell asleep.

The woman ran to fetch her husband. The man entered the room and quietly approached the sleeping giant. He stabbed one of the giant's necks with his sword and the giant awoke with a start. Groaning with pain, he leapt high into the sky and the man followed.

They fought high, high up in the clouds. The noise of their struggle sounded like thunder and when their swords clashed, great bolts of lightning struck the ground. The women below shook with fear and prayed with all their might.

Suddenly, one of the giant's heads came crashing down to the ground and then another. The heads cursed and rolled their eyes furiously. Then they sprang back into the sky and were rejoined to the giant's body.

As the furious battle continued, the young woman thought of a plan to help her husband. She and the maid-servant ran into the house and collected ashes from the hearth in their skirts. Then they ran back outside and waited.

Soon, another head came crashing to the ground but before it could spring back into the air, the women quickly smothered the neck with ashes. In a few minutes, the head closed its eyes

and died.

Eventually, the other eight heads fell to the ground and the women killed each one in the same way. Finally, the giant's huge body smashed to earth with a tremendous thud and he lay dead before them.

The man came down from the clouds to join his wife and the maid-servant and they joyously celebrated their wonderful victory.

The next morning, they found that the giant's great store-houses were brimming with gold, silver, rice and silk. They took the treasures and set off for home. On the way, they tried to find the helpful old woman in order to share their good fortune with her. But she was nowhere to be found so they went home to their village and lived happily ever after.

the toad bridegroom

Once upon a time there lived a poor fisherman and his wife. He went fishing in the lake every day, but one summer the water in the lake began to dry up and, with each passing day, he caught fewer and fewer fish.

One day, he went to the lake and the water was completely gone. Instead, a big ugly toad sat on the bottom of the lake. The fisherman thought that the toad had eaten all of the fish and cursed him angrily. The toad hopped up to the fisherman and said, "Please don't be angry with me. I haven't eaten the fish. The lake is gone now and I have no place to live. Please take me home with you." The man was horrified at the thought and went home, leaving the toad behind.

That night, the toad came to the fisherman's house and asked again, "Please let me live in your home and I will bring

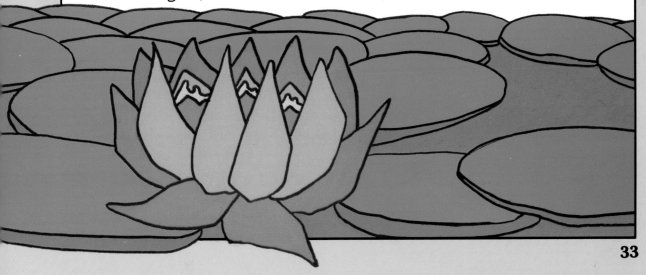

you good fortune." The man told the toad to go away but his wife begged him to let the toad stay, for they had no children and she thought that the toad would make a good pet. Her husband finally agreed and she made a bed for the toad in a corner of the kitchen and fed him worms and rice.

In time, the man and his wife came to love the toad as if it were their own son and he grew as big as a young man. One day, the toad told them, "I would like to marry soon. Your neighbor is a rich man with three daughters. Please try to arrange for me to marry one of them."

The man and his wife were very upset by the toad's request for, even though they loved him very much, after all he was not a human being. But the toad finally persuaded them to go to the rich man's house and make the proposal.

They went to their neighbor's house and nervously told them of the toad's desire to marry one of their daughters. The rich man and his wife were so angered by such a preposterous request that they ordered their servant to beat the fisherman and his wife and send them away.

They went home and sadly told the toad what had happened. "I'm sorry you've been treated so badly, Mother and Father," he said, "but wait and see. I'll make everything all right."

That night, the toad caught a hawk and tied a lantern to its foot with a long string. He took the hawk to the rich man's house and climbed a tall persimmon tree. The toad lit the lantern and said in a loud voice, "Today, the master of this house rejected a proposal of marriage. I shall give you one more day to reconsider your decision. Otherwise, great doom will fall upon your household."

The rich man was wakened by the toad's proclamation and rushed to his window. As he looked out, the toad released the hawk and the bird flew away with the glowing lantern trailing behind. The man was frightened by the light glowing in the sky and was convinced that he had received a message from the Heavenly King.

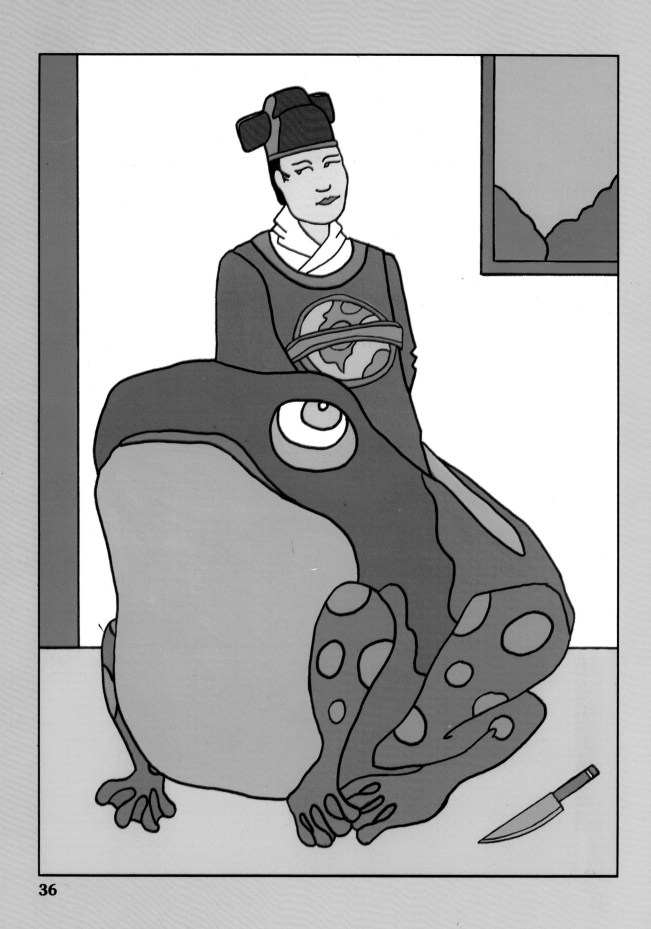

The next morning, he gathered his daughters together and told them of the terrible fate in store for their family. The first and second daughters were furious and each refused the marriage proposal. But the youngest daughter was a filial girl and agreed to marry the ugly toad in order to save her family from destruction.

Thus the marriage was arranged and the wedding was attended by a great number of people from far and near who were curious to see such a bizarre sight.

The young bride was quite miserable at the thought of spending the rest of her life with the toad but she knew it was her duty to her family and behaved with great dignity throughout the ceremony, never letting her misery be known. After the wedding, the guests made rude jokes and laughed at the repulsive toad but he and his bride took no notice of their cruelty.

When the celebration was over, the young couple went to the bridal chamber. The bride quietly sat down in a corner of the room and, as she looked at the ugly toad who was now her husband, a small tear trickled down from her eye. The toad looked at his bride and said, "Don't be afraid. You have proved yourself to be a girl of great worth. Now do as I say. Bring a knife and cut the skin from my back."

The girl was greatly shocked by his request but she did as he asked. She made a long cut in the skin of his back and, to her great surprise, out stepped a handsome young prince!

The next morning, the prince put his toad skin on again and the couple went outside. The crowd of wedding guests was waiting with great curiosity and the people were astonished to see the young bride happy and smiling.

As the crowd gathered around them, the prince stepped out of his toad skin and revealed his true self to the startled people. Then he took his bride and his parents away to live in a beautiful palace and they all lived happily ever after.

the
magic
mallet

Long, long ago when tigers smoked their pipes on the mountaintop, there lived a very poor family. The father was too sick to work so the eldest son went to the mountains every day to cut firewood. His mother sold the wood he gathered in order to buy food for the family.

As he was cutting wood late one afternoon, the boy felt hungry. By good fortune, he found a walnut tree in the forest and climbed it. He picked the nuts and ate until he was full. But he was a thoughtful boy and for every nut he ate, he gathered one for his father, one for his mother, one for his brother and one for his sister. He put them in his sack and started for home.

The boy came to a small shrine by the side of the path and, since it was growing dark, decided to spend the night there. It was empty and dark inside. The boy felt frightened but he was very tired, so he crept up into the rafters and soon fell asleep.

In the middle of the night, he was awakened by a great hubbub outside. As he peeked down from the rafters, a crowd of goblins rushed inside. They sat down and talked excitedly with one another.

"What did you do today?"

"I've been teasing a bad boy."

"I spent the day swinging on the tail of an ox."

"I sat on top of a gentleman's horsehair hat."

"I've been dancing under a floor."

"I played in a ditch and blew bubbles in the mud."

They continued their lively conversation until each had told how he had spent the day. Then the head goblin said, "Now it is time to eat," and he took a mallet from his belt.

He struck the mallet on the floor and said, "Tu-du-rag-tag-tag, come out rice." Suddenly a great bowl of rice appeared. He struck the mallet again and chanted, "Tu-du-rag-tag-tag, come out wine." At once, a cask of wine appeared. The goblin continued striking the mallet on the floor. Many delicious things appeared and the goblins feasted merrily.

As the boy watched quietly from the rafters, he began to feel hungry too. He took a walnut from his sack and cracked it between his teeth. The noise frightened the goblins and they shouted, "The roof is falling down! Let's get out of here!" They all rushed out and ran away, leaving behind the food and the mallet.

The boy cautiously climbed down from the rafters. The goblins were nowhere to be seen so he sat down and ate until he thought he would burst. Then he picked up the mallet and struck it on the floor, saying, "Tu-du-rag-tag-tag, come out clothes." Immediately, a suit of fine clothes appeared. Then he wished for a pair of shoes in the same way. The shoes appeared and the boy was convinced that this was indeed the magic mallet of legendary fame.

At daybreak, the boy ran home with the mallet as fast as he could and his family rejoiced at their good fortune.

But, in the same village, there lived a very selfish boy. When

he heard of the sudden wealth of the woodcutter's family, he went to their house and asked the boy about the secret of his great luck. The boy told his friend what had happened in the forest.

The selfish boy ran into the mountains and found the walnut tree. He quickly picked some nuts and put them into his sack. Then he ran to the shrine and climbed up into the rafters.

In the middle of the night, the goblins came in. The head goblin struck a mallet on the floor and the feast began. But the selfish boy was too impatient to wait until the goblins were groggy from the wine. He took a walnut from the sack and cracked it between his teeth.

But this time the goblins were not frightened. They shouted, "There is the mischievous boy who tricked us!" and they dragged him down from the rafters.

"What shall we do with this greedy fellow?" asked the head goblin.

"Beat him!" replied one.

"Hang him!" said another.

The head goblin thought for a few moments and said, "No. After all, he's only a boy. I think we should just stretch his tongue." The others agreed. The head goblin struck the boy's tongue with his mallet, saying, "Tu-du-rag-tag-tag, come out tongue, one-hundred feet long." The boy's tongue started to grow and it did not stop until it was a hundred feet long. The goblins sent him away and the poor boy staggered along, carrying his tongue on his back. Exhausted, he collapsed on a river bank.

He thought for a long, long time. Feeling great remorse for his selfishness, he decided that he must change his ways and try to help others. He saw that there was no way for travelers to cross the river so he stretched his tongue to the other side to serve as a bridge. Everyone who crossed the bridge was most appreciative and the boy was glad to be of service. But, needless to say, he was miserable to think that he would be in such a state for the rest of his life.

Back in the village, the woodcutter boy heard about the terrible fate which had befallen his friend and he went off to rescue him. He wandered through the mountains and eventually came to the river and saw his friend with his tongue stretched across it.

The boy crossed the river on the tongue-bridge and approached his friend. The selfish boy cried, "I have repented of my evil-minded ways but now I'm stuck here forever."

"I shall try to help you," replied the kind lad.

He took the magic mallet from his belt and, striking the gigantic tongue, said, "Tu-du-rag-tag-tag, tongue, draw back in." At once, the enormous tongue shrank back into the boy's mouth and became its normal size.

The boys returned to their village and the selfish boy was so grateful that he never did another selfish thing again as long as he lived.

46

the tiger and the rabbit

One day, many years ago, a tiger roamed the hills looking for something to eat. By chance, he met up with a young rabbit.

"I'm going to eat you for breakfast," he told the rabbit.

"Mr. Tiger, I'm too small and skinny to make a good meal," replied the rabbit. "Let me fix you some special rice cakes. I'll even make a fire and toast them for you."

The sly rabbit collected some small white stones and showed them to the tiger. "How do you eat them?" asked the tiger.

"It's very simple," the rabbit answered. "We'll toast them over the fire until they become red hot. You can't imagine how delicious they are."

The rabbit collected some twigs and started a fire. Then he put the stones on the fire and said, "Mr. Tiger, there are ten rice cakes—five for each of us. I'm going to get some bean sauce to eat with them. It will make them ever so much tastier. But please don't eat any until I get back."

The rabbit scampered away as the tiger watched the stones glowing in the fire. He licked his lips with anticipation and counted the stones.

"The rabbit said there were ten rice cakes but actually there are eleven," he said to himself. "If I eat one now, he'll never know the difference."

He took the reddest one from the fire and popped it into his mouth and swallowed it with one gulp. Of course, it was so hot that it burned his mouth and tongue, his throat and his stomach, too. He ran back to his cave in pain and could not eat anything for a whole month.

After he recovered, the tiger went out one day looking for something to eat and by chance met up with the same young rabbit. "You scoundrel!" he shouted. "You tricked me and I suffered terribly. I'm really going to eat you now."

The rabbit trembled with fear but calmly said, "Please don't be angry with me, Mr. Tiger. Look, I've found a way to catch hundreds and hundreds of sparrows. If you will sit still and look at the sky with your mouth open, I'll drive them into your mouth and they will make a wonderful feast."

The tiger looked about and saw thousands of sparrows in the sky and he licked his lips with anticipation. But he remembered what had happened the last time and asked, "How can I trust you? Are you trying to trick me again?"

"Of course not, Mr. Tiger," replied the rabbit. "Just do what I say. Go and sit in the middle of the bushes and I'll chase the sparrows into your mouth."

The tiger did as he was told. Looking at the sky, he sat down and opened his mouth. The rabbit quietly set fire to the bushes and said, "Don't move, Mr. Tiger, they're starting to come your way now." Then he quickly scampered away.

The crackling of the burning bushes sounded like the twittering of sparrows to the tiger and he waited patiently. Suddenly, he realized that it was getting very hot indeed. He looked around and, to his surprise, he was completely surrounded by a raging fire and barely managed to escape. All of his fur was burned to a frazzle and he had to stay in his cave for months until it grew back.

One winter morning, the tiger went out looking for something to eat and by chance he met up again with the very same young rabbit.

"You miserable wretch!" he roared. "You've tricked me twice and I'm going to eat you up this very instant."

"Mr. Tiger, you don't understand," said the rabbit. "I was

trying to help you but you didn't follow my instructions. Now look here—there are wonderful fat fish swimming in the river. You won't believe how tasty they are."

The tiger was curious. "How do you catch them?" he asked.

"With your tail, Mr. Tiger. It will make a splendid fishing pole," answered the rabbit.

"You had better not try to trick me again," the tiger said. "This is your last chance."

"Just trust me," said the rabbit, "and remember the old proverb that says, 'If you try three times, you will meet with success.' Now come over to the river bank and dip your tail in the water. You must sit very still and close your eyes."

The tiger licked his lips with anticipation and did as he was told. The rabbit waded to the other side of the river and shouted, "I'm chasing the fish over to your tail. The water is very cold but remember to keep still. Soon your tail will be heavy with fish." Then the rabbit scampered away.

After darkness fell, it became very cold and the river began to freeze. The tiger moved his tail a tiny bit and it felt very heavy. "Good," he said to himself. "I've already caught lots of fish. In just a little while longer I'll have even more."

Around midnight, the tiger said, "Well, I think I've caught loads of fish by now. It's time to eat." He started to pull his tail out of the river and discovered that it was frozen fast. He pulled and pulled with all his might but he could not free his tail.

Early the next morning, a hunter passed by and caught the tiger and carried him away. And that is one greedy old tiger who will never again be a worry to rabbits.

the magic pumpkins

It is told that two brothers once lived in a small village and they were as different from one another as night is from day.

The elder brother, Nolbu, was an ill-tempered, horrid man who would make children cry and even throw rocks at people's *kimchi* pots. Even worse, Nolbu had cheated his younger brother out of all the family's wealth, so that he and his wife lived in splendor while his brother's family was forced to live in poverty.

The younger brother, Hungbu, was a good and gentle man. He lived in a small mud hut with his wife and nine children and they were so poor that their clothes were made from old rice sacks and they hardly had enough food to survive. But Hungbu never complained about his misfortune and, even though his brother had swindled him, bore no ill feelings toward him.

During the winter, Hungbu's family slept on tattered straw mats on the cold earth floor and huddled together to keep warm. Each day, he worked from dawn to dusk gathering wood and weaving straw sandals to sell. In this way, he barely managed to keep his family alive.

One day, there was not a grain of rice left so Hungbu went to Nolbu's fine house. "Honorable brother, I'm sorry to bother you but my family has nothing to eat. Can you please help us?" he begged.

Nolbu's storehouse was brimming with rice but the selfish man refused to help his brother, saying, "I have only enough for my own household. Go away!"

Poor Hungbu left empty-handed and had to sell his shoes on the way home in order to buy some rice for his family. And thus they struggled through the winter.

At long last, spring arrived and the swallows returned from the south. They built their nests in the rafters of Hungbu's house and the air was filled with their happy singing.

One day, Hungbu was weaving sandals outside and a baby swallow fell from its nest to the ground. He rushed over to the tiny bird and saw that its leg was broken. "Oh, you poor little thing! Please let me help you," he said.

He took the bird inside his house and carefully bound the broken leg. The children took turns feeding insects to it and nursed the little bird back to health. Finally the leg was mended although it would always be a bit crooked.

Summer passed and it was autumn once again. When the days grew short and frost covered the ground, it was time for the swallows to fly south for the winter. As they left, the young bird with the crooked leg chirped goodbye to his friend, Hungbu.

After a long, cold winter, spring came again and the swallows gladly returned to their old home. As the family welcomed them, the bird with the crooked leg perched on

Hungbu's shoulder and dropped a seed into his hand. "How curious," he thought. "Let's plant it right away and see what grows."

What Hungbu could not know was that this was no ordinary seed but a magic one, sent to him by the King of the Swallows as a reward for saving the baby bird.

The seed sprouted and grew into a thick vine which climbed all the way up to the roof of the house. On the vine bloomed three large white flowers with a fragrance sweeter than any other blossoms in the land.

By autumn, three enormous pumpkins grew on the vine. Hungbu was filled with joy, for they were large enough to feed his family throughout the winter.

One day, Hungbu said to his wife, "The pumpkins have ripened. It's time to harvest them." The whole family went to help. With great difficulty, they cut down the pumpkins and laid them on the ground in a row.

Hungbu took his saw and started to cut the first pumpkin. As he did, it exploded with a bang and out came an endless stream of rice—enough to feed his family for the rest of their lives!

The second pumpkin split open and out poured great quantities of gold and silver and the finest silk.

From the third pumpkin came carpenters with tools and timbers. In an instant, they built a splendid house filled with the finest furniture.

The family could hardly believe their eyes. To their great surprise, Hungbu was now the richest man in the province!

They lived happily and Hungbu gladly shared his wealth with all those in need and was greatly loved by the people.

One day, Nolbu heard the news of his brother's great fortune. Overcome by jealousy and greed, he rushed to Hungbu's house and asked him the secret of his success. Without hesitation, Hungbu told him all about the swallow and the pumpkins. Nolbu hurried off without even a word of thanks.

On the way home, Nolbu stole a baby swallow from its nest

and took it home. The wicked man broke the tiny bird's leg and then bound it up, saying, "Your leg will heal soon, little bird. Don't forget how I've helped you."

In due time, the bird's leg mended and it flew south for the winter with the rest of the swallows. When they returned in the spring, the bird found Nolbu and deposited a seed in his hand. He jumped for joy and said to himself, "Soon I'll be the richest man in the province!" He hastily planted the seed. "Hurry up and grow," he said.

The seed sprouted and grew into a thick vine. Three huge red flowers bloomed and, although they had a loathsome smell, Nolbu and his wife were too busy thinking about how rich they would be to notice the terrible odor.

By autumn, three great pumpkins had ripened on the vine. Nolbu rubbed his hands together greedily—it was now time for the harvest.

He started to cut open a pumpkin and out popped a money collector. "I have a list of every person you've ever cheated," he said. "Now you must repay them ten times over." Nolbu was quite dismayed but he thought of the riches which he would surely find in the other two pumpkins. He led the collector to his money chest and paid what was demanded. The list was very long and, by the time he finished, the chest was empty.

Nolbu hurried back to the pumpkins. "I'm sure this one is loaded with gold and silver," he thought as he cut it open. But to his great surprise, out jumped a hoard of demons. "You're a selfish, evil man!" they shouted. "This will teach you a lesson," and they beat him with their clubs until he was black and blue all over.

Struggling back to his feet, Nolbu thought, "There's still one pumpkin left. It's bound to be filled with treasure." He cut open the last pumpkin but instead of riches, out spewed great clouds of smoke and scorching flames. The flames shot out in every direction and the fire did not stop until every single bit of his property was burned to the ground.

Nolbu and his wife cried with anguish. "I am ruined! What

can we do?" he asked. "Your brother is a good man. Perhaps he will help us," she answered.

They went to Hungbu's house and were welcomed with open arms. Hungbu gave half of everything he owned to his brother. Nolbu was so touched by his brother's kindness and generosity that he at once became a good and humble man and they all lived happily together forever after.